D0475567

To Andrea

Hey Otter! Hey Beaver!
Copyright © 2023 by Brian Pinkney
All rights reserved. Manufactured in Italy.
For information address HarperCollins Children's Books,
a division of HarperCollins Publishers, 195 Broadway, New York, NY 10007.
www.harpercollinschildrens.com

The full-color art was painted with India ink, opaque watercolor,
and acrylics on Strathmore watercolor paper.
The text type is 22-point Billy.

Library of Congress Cataloging-in-Publication Data

Names: Pinkney, J. Brian, author, illustrator.
Title: Hey Otter! Hey Beaver! / written and illustrated by Brian Pinkney.
Description: First edition. | New York : Greenwillow Books,
an Imprint of HarperCollins Publishers, [2023] | Audience: Ages 4-8. |
Audience: Grades K-1. | Summary: "Good friends Otter and Beaver use
water and sticks for very different purposes as they spend time together"
—Provided by publisher.
Identifiers: LCCN 2022004312 | ISBN 9780063159822 (hardcover)
Subjects: CYAC: Otters—Fiction. | Beavers—Fiction. |
Animals—Habits and behavior—Fiction. | LCGFT: Animal fiction. | Picture books.
Classification: LCC PZ7.P63347 He 2023 | DDC [E]—dc23
LC record available at https://lccn.loc.gov/2022004312
23 24 25 26 27 RTLO 10 9 8 7 6 5 4 3 2 1
First Edition
Greenwillow Books

Hey OTTER! Hey BEAVER!

Brian Pinkney

Greenwillow Books
An Imprint of HarperCollins Publishers

"Hey, Beaver!" said Otter.
"The water is flowing. Let's play!"

"Hey, Otter," said Beaver.

"Look, flowing water! Let's get to work."

Otter and Beaver
jumped into the stream.

"I love to play with sticks," said Otter.
"I love to build with them," said Beaver.
Otter and Beaver dove for a stick
at the same time.

But Otter got there first.

"Hey, Otter, give me that stick!" said Beaver. "I need that stick. I really really really really need that stick to build my dam."

"But Beaver," said Otter.
"I'm spinning
this stick.
I'm balancing
this stick.
Now I'm tossing
this stick.
It's time to play!"

Beaver grabbed the stick
right out of the air.
"Thanks, Otter!" he said,
slapping his tail.

"Keep the stick," said Otter. "I see branches."

"I love to build with branches," said Beaver.
   They dove for the branches
   at the same time.

But Otter got there first.

"I'm balancing these branches.
I'm spinning these branches.
Watch me toss these branches."

"What beautiful branches these are!" said Otter.

"Hey, Otter," said Beaver.
"Give me those branches. I need those branches.
  Please give me give me give me
  those branches right now!"

Beaver snatched them out of the air.
"Thanks, Otter," he said, slapping his tail.

"I place one on the left. I place one on the right.
'Cause I'm building a dam, such a beautiful dam."

"Hey, Beaver," said Otter.
"I'm floating like a log
just floating like a log
a big sturdy log am I."

"*Hmmm,*" said Beaver, looking around.
"I could use a log."

"I am the log!" said Otter.

"Hey, Otter, silly Otter," said Beaver.

"You can't be part of my dam."

"Hey, Beaver," said Otter. "What about twigs?
Can you use twigs? I found these twigs!"

"Oh, yes. Give me those twigs.
I need those twigs.
Please pass me pass me pass me
those twigs," said Beaver.
"My beautiful dam needs twigs."

"Hey, Beaver," said Otter. "You used up all the sticks, branches, and twigs, and now there is nothing to play with and no more flowing water!"

"A job well done!" said Beaver.

"I'll just take one back," said Otter.

"Thanks!"
said Otter.

"Uh-oh," said Beaver.

"We can spin another stick, Otter," said Beaver.

"We can build another dam, Beaver," said Otter.

Otter and Beaver dove for a stick
in the flowing stream.